The Little Prince

ANTOINE DE SAINT-EXUPÉRY

Translated by Joseph Laredo

This edition published in 2017 by Arcturus Publishing Limited
26/27 Bickels Yard, 151–153 Bermondsey Street,
London SE1 3HA

Design copyright © Arcturus Holdings Limited

For this Arcturus edition:
Design: Jeni Child
Cover design: Michael Reynolds
Project management: Frances Evans
Proofreading: Tracey Kelly

ISBN: 978-1-78428-424-4
CH005442UK
Supplier 09, Date 1017, Print run 6623

Printed in the UK

TO LÉON WERTH

Children, please forgive me for dedicating this book to a grown-up. I have a very good excuse: this particular grown-up is my best friend in all the world. I have another excuse: this particular grown-up understands everything – even children's books. I have a third excuse: this particular grown-up lives in France, where he is cold and hungry and needs comforting. If all these excuses aren't good enough, I am happy to dedicate this book to the child this particular grown-up once was. All grown-ups began life as children (though few of them remember this). I therefore amend my dedication as follows:

TO LÉON WERTH,
WHEN HE WAS A LITTLE BOY

CHAPTER ONE

One day, when I was six, I saw a wonderful picture. It was in a book on primeval forests called *True Stories* and it showed a boa constrictor about to swallow a big cat. This is a copy of the picture.

In the book it said: 'Boa constrictors swallow their prey whole, without chewing it. After that, they can't move and they sleep for six months, which is the time it takes them to digest it.'

That made me think about all the exciting things that could happen in a jungle, and, eventually,

I drew a picture of my own, using coloured pencils. It was my first drawing, Drawing Number One, and it looked like this:

I showed my masterpiece to some grown-ups and asked them if they found the drawing scary.

They said, 'Why should a hat be scary?'

But my drawing wasn't of a hat. It was of a boa constrictor digesting an elephant. So I drew another picture showing the inside of the boa constrictor, so that grown-ups could understand. They always need things explained. Drawing Number Two looked like this:

The grown-ups advised me to stop drawing boa constrictors, with or without their insides showing, and to concentrate instead on geography, history, arithmetic and grammar. Which was how, at the age of six, I abandoned a glittering career as an artist. The failure of Drawings Number One and Two had put me off. Grown-ups can never understand anything by themselves, and children get tired of having to explain everything.

So I had to choose another career, and I became a pilot. I flew all over the world. And geography did indeed come in very handy. I could tell at a glance whether I was over China or Arizona – which is very useful if you get lost in the dark.

During my life as a pilot, I met lots of people – lots of serious people. I spent a great deal of time with grown-ups. I studied them very closely. It didn't improve my opinion of them much.

Whenever I met any who seemed intelligent, I tested them by showing them Drawing Number One, which I always kept with me. I wanted to know whether they could really understand things. But they always said, 'It's a hat.' So I didn't talk to them about boa constrictors or primeval forests or the stars. I kept to things they could grasp. I talked about bridge and golf and politics and ties. And the grown-ups were very happy to have met someone so sensible.

CHAPTER TWO

And so I lived alone, with no one I could really talk to, until six years ago, when I broke down over the Sahara Desert. Part of my engine had failed. And, since I had neither a mechanic nor any passengers with me, I had to face making a difficult repair all by myself. I knew it was a matter of life or death. I had barely enough drinking water to last a week.

So, that night, I slept on the sand a thousand miles from anywhere. I was even more cut off than if I had been adrift on a raft in the middle of the ocean. You can imagine my surprise, then, when I was woken in the morning by a strange little voice.

It said, 'Please, sir … draw me a lamb!'

'Eh?'

'Draw me a lamb.'

I leapt to my feet as if I had been struck by lightning. I rubbed my eyes and looked around. And I saw the most extraordinary little fellow, studying me earnestly. I tried to draw him later, and this is the best I could manage. But, of course, my drawing is much less striking than the real thing. It isn't my fault. I had been put off making a career as an artist by grown-ups when I was six, and

I had never learned to draw anything – except boa constrictors with and without their insides showing.

So I stared at this apparition in wide-eyed astonishment. Don't forget that I was a thousand miles from anywhere. Yet the little fellow before me didn't seem to be lost, nor dying of exhaustion, nor dying of hunger or thirst, nor frightened to death. He didn't look anything like a child lost in the middle of the desert, a thousand miles from anywhere.

When I finally managed to speak, I said, 'But … what are you doing here?'

And again he said, very softly, as if it was a matter of the greatest importance, 'Please, sir … draw me a lamb.'

When you are confronted by such a powerful mystery, you don't dare disobey. Absurd as it seemed, since I was a thousand miles from anywhere and in mortal danger, I put my hand in my pocket and took out a piece of paper and a pen. But then I remembered that I had studied mostly geography, history, arithmetic and grammar, and I told the little fellow (with some frustration) that I couldn't draw.

He replied, 'Never mind. Draw me a lamb.'

As I had never drawn a lamb before, I drew him one of the only two things I knew how to draw – the boa constrictor without its insides showing.

And I was astonished to hear the little fellow say, 'No! No! I don't want a picture of an elephant inside a boa constrictor. Boa constrictors are very dangerous, and elephants take up a lot of space. My home is very small. I need a lamb. Draw me a lamb.'

So I drew one.

He watched me attentively.

Then he said, 'No! That one's already on its last legs. Draw me another one.'

I drew another one.

My new friend smiled politely and patiently.

'You know very well that isn't a lamb. It's a ram. It's got horns …'

So I did yet another drawing, but this one was rejected as well.

'That one's too old. I want a lamb that lives a long time.'

By now I was running out of patience, as I was anxious to start dismantling my engine, so I quickly drew this.

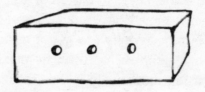

And I snapped, 'That's its box. The lamb you wanted is inside it.'

And I was amazed to see my young critic's face light up.

'That's just the kind of lamb I wanted! Do you think it'll need lots of grass?'

'Why?'

'Because my home is very small ...'

'I'm sure there'll be enough. I've given you a very small lamb.'

He looked down at the drawing.

'Not that small ... Look! He's gone to sleep ...'

And that is how I met the little prince.

CHAPTER THREE

It took me a long time to work out where he had come from. Although he asked me lots of questions, the little prince never took any notice of mine. So it was from things he just happened to mention that I gradually pieced it all together. For example, when he first saw my plane (I shan't draw my plane; it's far too complicated for me to draw), he said, 'What's that thing there?'

'It's not a thing. It can fly. It's an plane. It's my plane.'

And I was proud to tell him that I could fly.

Then he exclaimed, 'What! You've fallen from the sky?'

'Yes,' I said, modestly.

'Ha! That's funny …'

And the little prince burst into joyful laughter, which I found very annoying. I like people to take my misfortunes seriously.

Then he added, 'So you come from the sky as well! Which planet are you from?'

I immediately spotted a glimmer of light in the mystery of his presence in the desert, and I quickly asked, 'So you're from another planet?'

But he didn't answer me. He was gently nodding in the direction of my plane.

'It's true, you couldn't have come very far in that.'

And he lapsed into a lengthy daydream. Then, taking my lamb from his pocket, he sank into a profound meditation on his prize.

You can imagine how much his veiled reference to other planets had intrigued me. So I was eager to find out more.

'Where do you come from, little fellow? Where is "your home"? Where are you taking my lamb?'

After a thoughtful silence, he said, 'The good thing about the box you've given me is that, at night, he'll be able to sleep in it.'

'That's right. And if you like, I'll also give you a rope to tie him up with during the day. And a post.'

My suggestion seemed to shock the little prince.

'Tie him up? What a strange idea!'

'But if you don't tie him up, he'll wander off somewhere and get lost …'

And my new friend burst out laughing again.

'But where do you think he'll go?'

'Wherever he likes. Whichever way he's facing.'

At that, the little prince said gravely, 'It won't make any difference. My home is so small!'

And, with a hint of sadness, he added, 'Whichever way you go, you can't get very far …'

CHAPTER FOUR

That was how I found out another very important thing about the little prince, which was that the planet he came from was not much bigger than a house!

I shouldn't have been too surprised. I knew very well that, apart from the large planets like Earth, Jupiter, Mars and Venus, which have been given names, there are hundreds of others, some so small that they can hardly be seen, even through a telescope. When astronomers discover one of these planets, they give it a number instead of a name. They call it, say, 'Asteroid 325'.

I have good reason to believe that the planet the little prince came from is Asteroid B612.

This asteroid has been seen only once, in 1909, through the telescope of a Turkish astronomer.

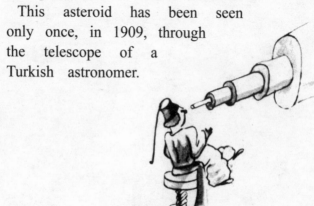

Soon afterwards, he proudly presented his discovery at an international astronomy congress. But no one believed him because of the way he was dressed. Grown-ups are like that.

Fortunately for Asteroid B612, a Turkish dictator then imposed the death penalty on anyone refusing to wear European-style clothes. The astronomer repeated his presentation in 1920, wearing a very elegant suit. And, this time, everyone believed him.

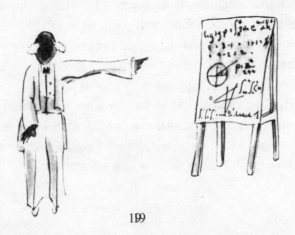

Why have I described Asteroid B612 in such detail and told you its number? Because of grown-ups. Grown-ups love numbers. When you tell them you have made a new friend, they never ask for the essential information. They never say, 'What's her voice like? What games does she like best? Does she collect butterflies?' They ask you, 'How old is she? How many brothers has she got? How much does she weigh? How much does her father earn?' This is how they believe they will get to know her. If you say to grown-ups, 'I've seen a beautiful house made of pink bricks, with geraniums in the windows and doves on the roof ...', they won't be able to visualize it. You need to say, 'I've seen a house worth a hundred pounds.'

Then they will exclaim, 'What a beautiful house!'

Similarly, if you say, 'The fact that the little prince was charming and wanted a lamb proves that he existed, because wanting a lamb proves that you exist', they will shrug their shoulders and treat you like a child! But if you say, 'He came from Asteroid B612,' they will believe you, and won't ask any more questions. That is how grown-ups are. There is no point in getting cross with them. Children have to be very tolerant with grown-ups.

But, of course, those of us who understand life couldn't care less about numbers! I wish I had begun this story like a fairy tale. I wish I could have written: 'Once upon a time, there was a little prince who lived on a planet hardly bigger than himself, and he needed a friend ...' Those who understand life would have found that much more believable.

You see, I don't want this book to be taken lightly. I find it quite distressing to write down what I remember. It is six years now since my little friend went off with his lamb. The reason I am writing about him is so that I don't forget him. It is sad to forget a friend. Some people have never had a friend. I don't want to become like those grown-ups who are only interested in numbers. That is why I bought a box of paints and coloured pencils. It is hard to start drawing again at my age, when all you have ever tried to draw is a boa constrictor, with and without its insides showing, at the age of six! I have, of course, tried to make my drawings as lifelike as possible, but I am not at all sure I have succeeded. One drawing is all right, and the next one looks nothing like him. The proportions are also a bit wrong. In one picture, the little prince is too big; in another, too small. I am not sure about the colours of his clothes, either. So I have tried this and that, and done the best I can. I might also have got more important details wrong. But you will have to forgive me for this. My little friend never explained anything. Perhaps he thought I was like him. But unfortunately, I can't see lambs through boxes. Perhaps I am a bit like a grown-up. I must have grown old.

CHAPTER FIVE

Every day, I found out something more about the little prince's planet, about why he left and how he got here. It happened quite gradually, as he remembered things. That was how, on the third day, I learned about the baobab problem.

This was also due to the lamb, because suddenly the little prince asked me, as if a terrible doubt had come over him, 'It is true, isn't it, that lambs eat bushes?'

'Yes. It's true.'

'Ah, I'm so glad!'

I couldn't understand why it should be so important that lambs eat bushes. But the little prince added, 'Therefore, they also eat baobabs?'

I pointed out to the little prince that baobabs are not bushes, but trees as tall as church towers, and

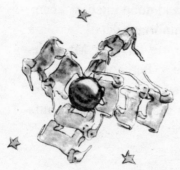

that, even if he took back a whole herd of elephants, they wouldn't be able to get through a single baobab.

The idea of taking back a herd of elephants made the little prince laugh.

'You'd have to stack them on top of each other …'
But then he spoke thoughtfully.

'Baobabs start out by being small, before they become tall.'

'That's right! But why do you want your lambs to eat small baobabs?'

He answered: 'Oh, that's a silly thing to ask!', as if the answer was obvious. And it took me a great deal of mental effort to work out the problem for myself.

In fact, on the little prince's planet, as on every other planet, there were good plants and bad plants. And consequently good plant seeds and bad plant seeds. But seeds aren't visible. They sleep secretly in the ground until one of them feels like waking up. Then it stretches and pushes up a lovely, harmless little shoot – tentatively at first – towards the sun. If it is a radish or a rose shoot, it can be left to grow freely. But if it is a bad plant, you must pull it up immediately, as soon as you realize what it is. Now, on the little prince's planet, there were some terrible seeds – baobab seeds. The planet's surface was infested with them. And baobabs, if they aren't tackled early enough, can never be got rid of. They take over the entire planet. Their roots penetrate it, and, if the planet is small and there are too many baobabs, they split it apart.

'It's just something you have to do,' the little prince told me later. 'Every morning, when you've finished cleaning yourself, you must carefully clean the planet. You have to make yourself pull up baobabs on a regular basis, as soon as you realize they aren't roses, they look just like roses when they're very small. It's a very tedious job, but a very simple one.'

And one day, he suggested I try to draw a picture good enough to put this message across to the children on Earth.

'If they ever go travelling,' he explained, 'they might find it useful. Sometimes, it's easy to put off things you have to do. But in the case of baobabs, it's always disastrous. On one planet I went to, the man who lived there was so lazy he'd let three of them grow ...'

From the little prince's description, I drew a picture of that planet. I don't really like telling people what they should and shouldn't do, but so few people know how dangerous baobabs can be. They pose such a threat to anyone finding themselves on an asteroid, that, for once, I made an exception. I am being honest and saying, 'Children! Beware of baobabs!' The reason I took so much trouble over this picture was that I wanted to warn my young friends of a risk they – like me – have been running for a long time without realizing it. The message I was giving them made it all worthwhile. You might wonder why there aren't any other drawings as elaborate as the drawing of the baobabs. The answer is simple: I tried but I failed. When I drew the baobabs, I was driven by a sense of urgency.

CHAPTER SIX

Ah, yes, my little prince, this is how, bit by bit, I came to know your sad story. For a long time, your only pleasure was watching the sun set. I discovered this new detail on the fourth morning, when you told me, 'I love sunsets. Let's go and see a sunset.'

'But we'll have to wait.'

'Wait for what?'

'For the sun to set.'

You were very surprised at first. Then you laughed at yourself and said, 'I forgot where I am – I always think I'm at home!'

When it is midday in the United States, as everyone knows, the sun is setting over France. If you could get to France in a minute or so, you would be able to watch the sunset. Unfortunately, France is much too far away. But on your tiny planet, all you had to do was move your chair a few inches, and you could watch the sun go down at any time you liked …

'One day, I saw the sun set forty-four times!'

And a little later, you added, 'You know, when you're as sad as I was, you love sunsets.'

'The day you watched forty-four of them, were you really that sad?'

But you didn't answer.

CHAPTER SEVEN

On the fifth day, again thanks to the lamb, another of the little prince's secrets was revealed to me.

He suddenly asked me, out of the blue, as if he had been silently mulling over the problem for some time, 'If lambs eat bushes, do they also eat flowers?'

'Lambs eat whatever comes their way.'

'Even flowers with thorns?'

'Yes. Even flowers with thorns.'

'So what's the use of thorns?'

I didn't know. I was right in the middle of trying to unscrew a jammed bolt in my engine. I was very worried – it was beginning to look as though there was a serious problem, and my drinking water was running out, making me fear the worst.

'What's the use of thorns?'

The little prince never let a question go once he'd asked it. But my bolt was annoying me, so I said the first thing that came into my head.

'Thorns are no use at all. They're just a flower's way of being nasty!'

'Oh!'

But after a moment's silence, he retorted, almost reproachfully, 'I don't believe you! Flowers are weak. They're also naive. They do their best to reassure themselves. They think their thorns make them terrifying …'

I didn't respond. At that moment, I was thinking, 'If this bolt won't unscrew, I'll smash it off with a hammer.' But the little prince broke my train of thought again.

'So do you think flowers …'

'No, I don't! I don't think anything! I said the first thing that came into my head. Unlike you, I have important things to worry about!'

He stared at me in amazement.

'Important things?'

He was looking at me. I had a hammer in my hand, my fingers were covered in grease and I was bent over an object that, to him, was extremely ugly.

'You sound like a grown-up!'

I felt a bit embarrassed. But he took no pity on me and continued, 'You confuse everything … you mix everything up!'

He was really very annoyed. His golden hair was shaking in the wind.

'I know a planet where there's a man with a bright red face. He has never smelled a flower. He has never gazed at a star. He has never loved anyone. He has never done anything but sums. And all day long he keeps saying, like you, "I'm an important man! I'm an important man!" And that makes him big-headed. But he isn't a man, he's a puffball!'

'A what?'

'A puffball!'

By now, the little prince was white with anger.

'For millions of years, flowers have been growing thorns. And for millions of years, lambs have been eating flowers anyway. But it isn't important to try to understand why flowers take so much trouble to grow thorns that are never of any use? It isn't important that lambs and flowers are at war? Isn't it more important than the sums the man with the red face does? And if I, the little prince, know of a flower that is the only one like it in the universe, that doesn't exist anywhere except on my planet, and that could be destroyed in one go by a lamb, one morning, just like that, without the lambs even realizing what it's doing, isn't that important, too?'

His face turned pink.

Then he went on, 'If someone loves a flower that's unique among all the millions of stars, that's all he needs to make him happy when he looks at them. He can say to himself, "My flower is up there somewhere …" But if the lamb eats the flower, for him, it's as if all the stars had suddenly gone out! But that's not important!'

He could find nothing more to say. Suddenly, he burst into tears. Night had fallen. I had put down my tools. I could no longer care about my hammer or my bolt, the fact that I had nothing to drink, or that I was going to die. There was a little prince on a planet, on my planet, Earth, who needed comforting! I took him in my arms. I rocked him. I said to him, 'The flower you love is not in danger … I'll draw a muzzle for your lamb … I'll draw you a shield for your flower … I'll …' I didn't really know what to say. I felt very clumsy. I didn't know how to reach him, how to connect with him … Sadness is such a mysterious place.

CHAPTER EIGHT

I very soon learned more about this flower. On the little prince's planet, there had always been very simple flowers, with a single row of petals, which didn't take up any space and didn't bother anyone. They appeared in the morning among the grass, and disappeared again in the evening. But one day, this flower emerged from a seed that had blown in from somewhere else. The little prince kept a close eye on the tiny shoot, which looked different from all the other tiny shoots. Perhaps it was a new species of baobab. But the plant soon stopped growing and started getting ready to flower. As he watched an enormous bud develop, the little prince was convinced that something miraculous was about to appear, but, hidden in her green cocoon, the flower simply continued preparing to be beautiful. She carefully chose her colours, she slowly put on her clothes and, one by one, she adjusted her petals. She didn't want to come out all crinkled like a poppy. She wanted to emerge resplendent in all her glory. Oh, yes! She was a very vain flower! So her secret preparations went on for days and days. And then, one morning, just as the sun came up, she revealed herself.

And, having worked so hard for so long, she yawned and said, 'Oh! I'm not even awake … Please excuse me … My hair's still a mess …'

But the little prince couldn't contain his delight.

'How beautiful you are!'

'Yes, aren't I?' replied the flower sweetly. 'And look, I've come out at the same time as the sun …'

The little prince realized that the flower was none too modest, but how good she made him feel!

'I do believe it's time for breakfast,' said the flower soon afterwards. 'Would you be kind enough to spare a thought for me?'

And the little prince was all embarrassed and went to fill a watering can with fresh water, which he sprinkled on the flower.

And so she was soon tormenting him with her vanity and capriciousness.

One day, for example, referring to her four thorns, she said to the little prince, 'Even tigers could not attack me with their claws … !'

'There aren't any tigers on my planet,' objected the little prince. 'In any case, tigers don't eat grass.'

'I'm not a grass,' replied the flower sweetly.

'Forgive me …'

'I may not be afraid of tigers, but I can't stand draughts. You wouldn't have a windbreak, would you?'

'A plant that can't stand draughts … what sort of a plant is that?' thought the little prince. 'This flower is much too complicated …'

'In the evenings, you're to put a dome over me. It's cold on your planet. It's not in a good location. Where I come from …'

But there she broke off. She had arrived as a seed. How could she have known anything about other worlds? Ashamed at being caught fabricating such a childish lie, she coughed two or three times, to make the little prince feel guilty.

'And the windbreak?'

'I was about to fetch it, but you were talking to me!'

Then she coughed a little harder to make him feel sorry anyway.

And so, despite wanting to show how much he loved her, the little prince soon became suspicious of the flower. He had taken her empty words seriously, and now he was very unhappy.

'I shouldn't have listened to her,' he confided in me one day. 'You should never listen to flowers. You should look at them and smell them. Mine filled my planet with fragrance, but I was unable to enjoy it. That business about the tigers should have made me feel sorry for her, but it only annoyed me ...'

He confided in me again another time.

'How stupid I was! I should have judged her on her actions and not on her words. She gave me her fragrance. She lit up my world. I should never have run away! I should have realized that her silly games were a sign of affection. Flowers are so full of contradictions! But I was too young to know how to love her.'

CHAPTER NINE

I think it was a flock of migrating birds that gave him an opportunity to get away. The morning before he left, he tidied the whole planet. First, he carefully swept his active volcanoes. He had two active volcanoes, which were really handy for heating his breakfast in the mornings. He also had a dormant volcano. But, as he always said, 'You never know!' So he swept the dormant volcano as well. If they're swept regularly, volcanoes burn gently and steadily, without ever erupting. Volcanic eruptions are like chimney fires. They are the result of neglect. Obviously, here on Earth our volcanoes are much too big for us to sweep. That is why they cause us so many problems.

Next, with some sadness, the little prince pulled up all the new baobab shoots. He thought he would never be going back. Yet, that morning, all these familiar tasks seemed unusually reassuring. And when he watered the flower for the last time and went to fetch the dome to put over her, he suddenly felt like crying.

'Goodbye,' he said to the flower.

But she didn't reply.

'Goodbye,' he said again.

The flower coughed – but not because she had a cold.

'I've been foolish,' she said at last. 'Please forgive me, and try to be happy.'

He was surprised that she hadn't reproached him. He stood there, with the dome at the ready, not knowing what to think. He couldn't understand why she was so kind and calm.

'Yes, I love you,' said the flower. 'You never knew. That was my fault. It really doesn't matter. But you were as foolish as I was. Try to be happy … Put the dome down. I don't want it any more.'

'But what about the wind?'

'My cough isn't as bad as all that … The cool night air will do me good. I'm a flower.'

'But what about the bugs and the animals?'

'If I can't put up with two or three caterpillars, how will I ever know what a butterfly is like? I hear they're very beautiful. In any case, who else will come and see me? You'll be a long way away. As for animals, I have nothing to fear. I have my own claws!'

And she innocently showed her four thorns.

Then she said, 'Don't stand around like that. It's annoying. You've decided to leave, so go.'

Because she didn't want him to see her cry. She was a very proud flower …

CHAPTER TEN

The little prince's planet was near Asteroids 325, 326, 327, 328, 329 and 330. So he started by visiting these in search of an occupation and in pursuit of knowledge.

The first of them was inhabited by a king. He was dressed in full regalia, all crimson and ermine, and sat on a very simple yet majestic throne.

'Ah! Here comes a subject!' exclaimed the king when he saw the little prince.

And the little prince thought, 'How can he know who I am when he has never seen me before?'

He didn't know that, for a king, things are very simple. Everyone is a subject.

'Come closer, so that I can see you better,' said the king, who was very proud to have someone to rule over.

The little prince looked around for somewhere to sit, but the entire planet was smothered by the king's magnificent ermine cloak. So he remained standing, and, being tired, he yawned.

'It is contrary to etiquette to yawn in the presence of a king,' said the monarch. 'I forbid it.'

'I can't help it,' replied the little prince with great embarrassment. 'I've had a long journey and I haven't slept …'

'In that case,' said the king, 'I command you to yawn. I haven't seen anyone yawn for years. Yawns are rather a rarity round here. Go ahead! Yawn again! I command you!'

'Now you're intimidating me … I can't do it again,' said the little prince, blushing deeply.

'Well now' replied the king, 'in that case, I… I command you sometimes to yawn and sometimes to …'

He mumbled something and seemed frustrated.

You see, for the king, the most important thing was that people should respect his authority. He could not tolerate disobedience. He was an absolute ruler. But since he was also a good man, he wanted his commands to be reasonable.

'If I were to command,' he continued, 'if I were to command a general to turn into a seabird, and if the general failed to obey, it would not be the general's fault. It would be my fault.'

'May I sit down?' asked the little prince timidly.

'I command you to sit down,' replied the king, majestically gathering up a corner of his ermine cloak.

But the little prince was amazed. The planet was minuscule. What could he possibly rule over?

'Your Majesty,' he said, 'please excuse me for asking, but ...'

'I command you to ask,' said the king hastily.

'Your Majesty ... what do you rule over?'

'Over everything,' replied the king plainly.

'Over everything?'

The king made a modest gesture that encompassed his own planet, the other planets and the stars.

'Over all that?' said the little prince.

'Over all that,' replied the king.

For not only was he an absolute ruler; he was also ruler of the universe.

'And do the stars obey you?'

'Of course,' said the king. 'They obey me instantly. I will not tolerate indiscipline.'

The little prince was amazed by the king's power. If it were his, he could watch not just forty-eight, but seventy-two or even a hundred or even two hundred sunsets in one day, without even having to move his chair! And as he was feeling rather sad at the thought of having abandoned his own planet, he decided to risk asking the king a favour.

'I'd like to see a sunset ... Would you be kind enough to command the sun to set?'

'If I were to command a general to fly from flower to flower like a butterfly, or to write a tragedy, or to turn into a seabird, and if the general failed to execute the command I had given him, which of us, he or I, would be at fault?'

'You would be,' said the little prince firmly.

'Precisely. One must ask of each person what that person can give,' continued the king. 'Authority rests primarily on reasonableness. If you command your people to go and throw themselves into the sea, they will revolt. I have the right to demand obedience because my commands are reasonable.'

'What about my sunset?' repeated the little prince, who never let a question go once he had asked it.

'You shall have your sunset. I shall demand it. But, in accordance with the science of government, I shall wait until the conditions are favourable.'

'When will that be?' enquired the little prince.

'Well now,' replied the king, consulting a large calendar, 'well now, it will be at about … at about … it will be this evening at about twenty minutes to eight! And you shall see how promptly I am obeyed.'

The little prince yawned. He was sorry he would miss the sunset, but he was getting rather bored.

'There's nothing more for me to do here,' he told the king. 'I'm going to move on!'

'Don't go!' replied the king, who was so pleased to have a subject. 'Don't go! I'll make you a minister!'

'A minister of what?'

'Of … of justice!'

'But there's no one to judge!'

'We don't know that,' said the king. 'I haven't yet been all round my kingdom. I am very old and walking tires me, but there is nowhere to keep a coach.'

'Oh, but I've already looked,' said the little prince, leaning over for another glance at the other side of the planet. 'There's no one over there, either …'

'Then you shall judge yourself,' replied the king. 'That is far more difficult. It is much more difficult to judge yourself than to judge others. If you can judge yourself properly, it means you have true wisdom.'

'But,' said the little prince, 'I can judge myself anywhere. I don't have to stay here.'

'Well now,' said the king, 'I do believe that somewhere on my planet there is an old rat. I hear it at night. You will be able to judge that. You will condemn it to death from time to time, so that its life depends on your judgment. But, each time, you will pardon it in the interest of practicality, as it is the only one.'

'But I don't like condemning things to death,' replied the little prince, 'and I really think I should be going.'

'No!' said the king.

But the little prince, who was now ready to depart, didn't want to upset the old king.

'If Your Majesty would like to be obeyed without hesitation, he might give me a reasonable command. He might command me, for example, to leave within one minute. It would seem that the conditions are favourable ...'

When the king did not reply, the little prince hesitated for a moment; then, with a sigh, he took off ...

'You shall be my ambassador,' cried the king hastily, with an air of great authority.

'Grown-ups are really strange,' said the little prince to himself, as he continued his journey.

CHAPTER ELEVEN

The second planet he came to was inhabited by a show-off.

'Aha! Here comes an admirer!' exclaimed the show-off, as soon as he saw the little prince approaching.

Because, to a show-off, other people are admirers.

'Hello,' said the little prince. 'What a funny hat you're wearing.'

'It's for raising,' replied the show-off. 'I raise it when I'm applauded. Sadly, no one ever comes this way.'

'Oh, really?' said the little prince, without understanding.

'Try clapping your hands,' suggested the show-off.

The little prince clapped his hands. The show-off raised his hat and gave a modest bow.

'This is more fun than being with the king,' thought the little prince. And he clapped his hands again. The show-off raised his hat again and gave another bow.

After five minutes of this monotonous game, the little prince was bored.

'And what do I need to do,' he asked, 'to make you drop your hat?'

But the show-off didn't hear him. Show-offs hear only praise.

'How much do you admire me?' he asked the little prince.

'What does "admire" mean?'

'It means to acknowledge that I am the handsomest, best dressed, richest and most intelligent person on the planet.'

'But you're the only person on your planet!'

'Be a good boy and admire me anyway!'

'I admire you,' said the little prince, shrugging his shoulders slightly, 'but what good will it do you?'

And the little prince flew off.

'Grown-ups really are very odd,' he said to himself as he continued his journey.

CHAPTER TWELVE

The next planet was inhabited by a drunkard. The little prince spent only a short time there, but it was enough to plunge him into a deep sadness.

'What are you doing?' he asked the drunkard, who was sitting in silence between a collection of empty bottles and a collection of full bottles.

'I'm drinking,' replied the drunkard dismally.

'Why are you drinking?' asked the little prince.

'To forget,' replied the drunkard.

'To forget what?' enquired the little prince, who already felt sorry for him.

'To forget that I'm ashamed,' confessed the drunkard, bowing his head.

'Ashamed of what?' asked the little prince, who wanted to help him.

'Ashamed of drinking!' concluded the drunkard, who then sank into silence as if there was nothing more to say.

And the little prince flew off, bewildered.

'Grown-ups really are very, very odd,' he said to himself as he continued his journey.

CHAPTER THIRTEEN

The fourth planet belonged to a businessman. He was such a busy man that he didn't even look up when the little prince landed.

'Hello,' said the little prince. 'Your cigarette has gone out.'

'Three plus two is five. Five plus seven is twelve. Twelve plus three is fifteen. Hello. Fifteen plus seven is twenty-two. Twenty-two plus six is twenty-eight. No time to relight it. Twenty-six plus five is thirty-one. Phew! That comes to five hundred and one million six hundred and twenty-two thousand seven hundred and thirty-one.'

'Five hundred million what?'

'Eh? You still here? Five hundred and one million … I can't remember … I'm too busy! I'm an important person, you know. I don't have time for idle chatter! Two plus five is seven …'

'Five hundred million what?' repeated the little prince, who had never in his life let a question go once he had asked it.

The businessman looked up.

'In the fifty-four years I've lived on this planet, I've only been disturbed three times. The first time

50

was twenty-two years ago, when a bug flew in from God knows where. It made such a dreadful noise I made four mistakes in one column. The second time was eleven years ago, when I had an attack of rheumatism. I'm an important person, you know. And the third time … was just now! Where was I? Yes, five hundred and one million …'

'Million what?'

The businessman realized he had no hope of being left in peace.

'Of those little things you sometimes see in the sky.'

'Flies?'

'No, no. Those little shiny things.'

'Bees?'

'No, no. Those little yellow things that idle people dream about. But I'm an important person, you know! I don't have time for day-dreaming.'

'Oh, you mean stars?'

'Yes, that's right. Stars.'

'And what are you going to do with five hundred million stars?'

'Five hundred and one million six hundred and twenty-two thousand seven hundred and thirty- one. I'm an important man, you know. I have to be precise.'

'And what are you going to do with all those stars?'

'What am I going to do with them?'

'Yes.'

'Nothing. I own them.'

'You own the stars?'

'Yes.'

'But I've just met a king who …'

'Kings don't own anything. They just "reign over" things. It's not the same at all.'

'And what's the point of owning the stars?'

'It makes me rich.'

'And what's the point of being rich?'

'So that I can buy other stars, if anyone finds any.'

'This man,' thought the little prince, 'is about as logical as the drunkard.'

Nevertheless, he kept on asking questions.

'How can you own the stars?'

'Who do you think they belong to?' retorted the businessman tetchily.

'I don't know. No one.'

'Then they belong to me, because I thought of it first.'

'Is that all you have to do?'

'Of course. If you find a diamond that doesn't belong to anyone, it's yours. If you find an island that doesn't belong to anyone, it's yours. If you have an idea that no one else has had, you patent it: it's yours. And I own the stars because no one else has ever thought of owning them.'

'That's true,' said the little prince. 'And what do you do with them?'

'I manage them. I count them. Then I count them again,' said the businessman. 'It's not easy. But I'm an important person!'

The little prince still wasn't satisfied.

'But if I own a scarf, I can put it around my neck and wear it. If I own a flower, I can pick it and take it somewhere. But you can't pick stars!'

'No, but I can bank them.'

'What does that mean?'

'It means that I write down on a piece of paper how many stars I own. Then I lock the piece of paper in a drawer.'

'Is that all?'

'That's all there is to it!'

'It might be amusing,' thought the little prince. 'It's also quite clever. But it's not very important.'

The little prince had very different ideas about what was important from those of grown-ups.

'Well,' he went on, 'I own a flower, which I water every day. I own three volcanoes, which I sweep every week. You see, I also sweep the dormant one. You never know. By owning my volcanoes and my flower, I can be of use to them. But you're of no use to the stars ...'

The businessman opened his mouth, but could think of nothing to say, and the little prince flew off.

'Grown-ups really are totally bizarre,' he said to himself as he continued his journey.

CHAPTER FOURTEEN

The fifth planet was very peculiar. It was the smallest of them all. There was just enough room on it for a street lamp and a lamplighter. The little prince could not comprehend what purpose could be served – here in the middle of the sky, on a planet without houses or people – by a street lamp and a lamplighter.

However, he said to himself, 'This man may be absurd, but he's less absurd than the king or the show-off or the businessman or the drunkard. At least what he does makes some sense. When he lights his lamp, it's as if he's creating a new star, or a new flower. When he puts out the lamp, the flower or the star goes to sleep. It's a beautiful occupation. It's truly useful because it's beautiful.'

When he landed on the planet, he greeted the lamplighter respectfully.

'Good morning. Why have you just put out your lamp?'

'It's my duty,' replied the lighter. 'Good morning.'

'What's your duty?'

'To put out my lamp. Good evening.'

And he lit it again.

'But why have you just lit it again?'

'It's my duty,' replied the lighter.

'I don't understand,' said the little prince.

'There's nothing to understand,' said the lighter. 'A duty is a duty. Good morning.'

And he put out his lamp.

Then he mopped his brow with a red-checked handkerchief.

'This is a terrible job. It was all right before. I put it out in the morning and lit it in the evening. The rest of the day I could relax, and the rest of the night I could sleep ...'

'So, since then, has your duty changed?'

'My duty hasn't changed,' said the lighter. 'That's the whole problem! The planet has revolved faster and faster each year, and the duty hasn't changed!'

'So?' said the little prince.

'So now that it revolves once a minute, I don't have a second's rest. I have to light it and put it out every minute!'

'How funny! Your days only last a minute!'

'It's not funny at all,' said the lighter. 'We've already been talking for a month.'

'A month?'

'Yes. Thirty minutes. Thirty days! Good evening.'

And he relit his lamp.

The little prince looked at him. He admired the lamplighter for doing his duty so diligently. He remembered the sunsets he used to go and see, by moving his chair. He wanted to help his new friend.

'You know … I've thought of a way you can rest whenever you like …'

'I always want to rest,' said the lighter.

For it is possible to be both diligent and lazy.

The little prince went on, 'Your planet is so small, you can walk around it in three strides. All you have to do is walk slowly and it will always be daytime. When you want a rest, you walk … and the day will last as long as you want it to.'

'That won't help me much,' said the lighter. 'What I like best is sleeping.'

'What a pity,' said the little prince.

'What a pity,' said the lamplighter. 'Good morning.'

And he put out his lamp.

'This one,' said the little prince to himself as he continued his journey, 'this one would be looked down on by all the others – the king, the show-off, the drunkard and the businessman. Yet he's the only one I don't find ridiculous. Perhaps that's because his occupation has to do with something other than himself.'

He gave a sigh of regret and said to himself, 'He's the only one I could have made friends with. But his planet is just too small. There's no room for us both …'

What the little prince couldn't bring himself to admit was that the thing he would miss most about this planet was that it was blessed with one thousand four hundred and forty sunsets every twenty-four hours!

CHAPTER FIFTEEN

The sixth planet was ten times as big. It was vast. And it was inhabited by an old man who wrote enormous books.

'Ah! Here comes an explorer!' he exclaimed when he saw the little prince.

The little prince sat down on the table and caught his breath for a moment. He'd travelled a long way by now!

'Where have you come from?' said the old man.

'What's that huge book?' said the little prince. 'What do you do here?'

'I'm a geographer,' said the old man.

'What's a geographer?'

'It's a clever person who knows the position of seas, rivers, towns, mountains and deserts.'

'That's really interesting,' said the little prince. 'At last,' he thought, 'a proper occupation!'

And he looked around him at the geographer's planet. He had never seen such a magnificent planet.

'It's really beautiful, your planet. Does it have any oceans?'

'I couldn't say,' said the geographer.

'Oh!' (The little prince was disappointed.) 'Or mountains?'

'I couldn't say,' said the geographer.

'Or towns or rivers or deserts?'

'I couldn't say that, either,' said the geographer.

'But you're a geographer!'

'That's right,' said the geographer, 'but I'm not an explorer. I don't know a single explorer. Geographers don't go out and find towns and rivers and mountains and seas and oceans and deserts. Geographers are much too important to swan around. They don't leave their offices. But they invite explorers in. They ask them questions, and they write down what they say they've seen. And if one of them says he has seen something that seems interesting, the geographer asks for a character check on the explorer.'

'Why is that?'

'Because if the explorer was lying, it would lead to huge errors in the geographer's books. The same thing would happen if the explorer drank too much.'

'Why is that?' asked the little prince.

'Because drunkards see double. So the geographer would record two mountains where there was only one.'

'I know someone,' said the little prince, 'who wouldn't be a very good explorer.'

'Quite possibly. So, if the explorer seems to be of good character, we then run a check on the thing he has discovered.'

'You go there?'

'No. That would be too complicated. We instruct the explorer to present some evidence. If, for example, he says he has discovered a large mountain, we instruct him to bring us some large rocks.'

The geographer suddenly became excited.

'But you've come a long way! You're an explorer! You can tell me about your planet!'

And the geographer, who had opened his record book, began sharpening his pencil.

'We write down the explorer's description in pencil first. We don't write it in ink until the explorer has presented his evidence …'

'Well?' said the geographer.

'Oh!' said the little prince. 'Well, my planet isn't all that interesting. It's very small. There are three volcanoes. Two active volcanoes and one dormant volcano. But you never know.'

'You never know,' said the geographer.

'There's also a flower.'

'We don't record flowers,' said the geographer.

'Why's that? They're beautiful, aren't they?

'Because flowers are ephemeral.'

'What does "ephemeral" mean?'

'Atlases,' said the geographer, 'are the most valuable of all books. They never go out of date. Mountains don't often move. Oceans very seldom run dry. The things we write about are eternal ...'

'But dormant volcanoes can wake up again,' interrupted the little prince. 'What does "ephemeral" mean?'

'Whether a volcano is asleep or awake makes no difference to us,' said the geographer. 'What matters to us is that it's a mountain. Mountains don't change.'

'But what does "ephemeral" mean?' repeated the little prince, who had never in his life let a question go once he had asked it.

'It means "having a very short life".'

'Will my flower have a very short life?'

'Of course.'

'My flower is ephemeral,' thought the little prince. 'And she has only four thorns to protect her against the world! And I've left her all alone on my planet!'

This was his first pang of conscience. But he pulled himself together.

'Where do you suggest I go next?' he asked.

'To the planet Earth,' answered the geographer. 'It is highly regarded ...'

And the little prince flew off, thinking about his flower.

CHAPTER SIXTEEN

So the seventh planet he visited was Earth.

Earth is no ordinary planet! It has a total of one hundred and eleven kings, seven thousand geographers, nine hundred thousand businessmen, seven-and-a-half million drunkards and three hundred and eleven million show-offs. Altogether, about two billion grown-ups.

To give you an idea of the size of Earth, let me tell you that, before electricity was invented, it had to support, counting all six continents, a veritable army of four hundred and sixty-two thousand lamplighters.

Seen from a certain distance, it created a marvellous effect. The advance of this great army was as precisely choreographed as a ballet. First on stage were the lighters in New Zealand and Australia. They then, having lit their lamps, went off to bed. Next to join the dance were the lighters in China and Siberia. Then they, too, slipped off into the wings. Next came the turn of the lighters in Russia and India. Then those in Africa and Europe. Then those in South America. Then those in North America. And not once did they come on at the wrong time. It was magnificent.

Only the lamplighter of the single lamp at the North Pole and his counterpart at the South Pole led easy, carefree lives: they only went to work twice a year.

CHAPTER SEVENTEEN

When you try to be funny, you sometimes bend the truth. I wasn't totally honest when I told you about the lamplighters, and I may have given anyone who doesn't know our planet a false impression. People take up only a very small part of Earth. If the two billion inhabitants that are spread across the planet stood side by side, as if they were at a rally, they would easily fit into a town square twenty miles long by twenty miles wide. The whole of humanity could be squeezed onto the smallest Pacific island.

Grown-ups, of course, won't believe you. They think they take up a lot of space. They think they're as big as baobabs. So you should suggest they work it out. They will enjoy it; they love numbers. But you mustn't waste your time on such a pointless exercise. You don't need to. Trust me.

When he arrived on Earth, the little prince was surprised to see no one about. He had begun to worry that he had gone to the wrong planet, when a moon-coloured coil stirred in the sand.

'Good evening,' said the little prince, just in case.

'Good evening,' said the snake.

'What planet have I landed on?' asked the little prince.

'On Earth, in Africa,' replied the snake.

'Oh! ... So there's no one on Earth?'

'This is the desert. There's no one in the desert. Earth is a big place,' said the snake.

The little prince sat down on a rock and looked up at the sky.

'I wonder,' he said, 'whether the stars shine so that we can all eventually find our way back to ours. Look, my planet's up there. It's directly above us ... But isn't it a long way away!'

'It's pretty,' said the snake. 'What are you doing here?'

'I'm having trouble with a flower,' said the little prince.

'Ah!' said the snake.

And neither of them spoke.

'Where are all the people?' asked the little prince at last. 'It's rather lonely in the desert ...'

'It's rather lonely among people, too,' said the snake.

The little prince looked at him for a while.

'You're a funny creature,' he said at last. 'As thin as my finger ...'

'But I'm more powerful than a king's finger,' said the snake.

The little prince smiled.

'You can't be that powerful ... You haven't even got any feet ... You can't even travel ...'

'I can take you further than any ship,' said the snake, and he wound himself around the little prince's foot, like a gold anklet.

'Whoever I touch is returned to the earth he came from,' he added. 'But you're pure and you've come from a star …'

The little prince said nothing.

'I feel sorry for you, a weak little thing on this great rock called Earth. I might be able to help you one day, if you ever miss your planet more than you can bear. I could …'

'Yes, yes, I understand,' said the little prince, 'but why do you always talk in riddles?'

'There are none that I cannot solve,' said the snake.

And neither of them spoke.

CHAPTER EIGHTEEN

The little prince crossed the desert and came across only a single flower. A flower with three petals, an insignificant flower …

'Hello,' said the little prince.

'Hello,' said the flower.

'Where are all the people?' asked the little prince politely.

The flower had once seen some nomads go by.

'People? There are six or seven of them, I think. I saw them a few years ago. But you never know where they might be. The wind blows them about. They don't have roots, which causes them lots of problems.'

'Goodbye,' said the little prince.

'Goodbye,' said the flower.

CHAPTER NINETEEN

The little prince climbed to the top of a large mountain. The only mountains he had ever seen were his three volcanoes, which came up to his knees. He used to use the dormant volcano as a stool. 'From the top of a mountain as high as this,' he thought, 'I'll be able to see the whole planet and all the people ...' But all he saw was sharply pointed rocks.

'Hello,' he said, just in case.

'Hello ... Hello ... Hello ...' answered the echo.

'Who are you?' said the little prince.

'Who are you? ... Who are you? ... Who are you? ...' answered the echo.

'Will you be my friends? I'm all alone,' he said.

'I'm all alone ... I'm all alone ... I'm all alone ...' answered the echo.

'What a funny planet!' thought the little prince. 'It's all dry and pointy and smells of salt.

'And the people have no imagination. They repeat everything you say to them ... On my planet, there was a flower – and she always spoke first ...'

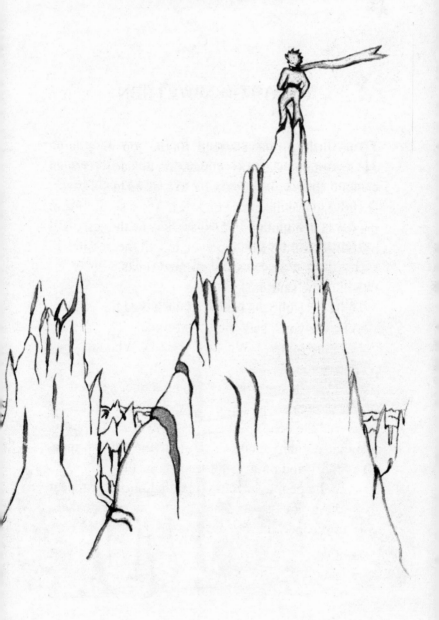

CHAPTER TWENTY

But finally, after walking for a very long time across sand, rocks and snow, the little prince came to a road. And roads always lead to people.

'Hello,' he said.

He was in a garden full of roses.

'Hello,' said the roses.

The little prince looked at them. They were all just like his flower.

'Who are you?' he asked, in disbelief.

'We're roses,' said the roses.

'Oh!' said the little prince …

And he felt very unhappy. His flower had told him she was the only one of her kind in the universe. And here were five thousand others, all just the same, in a single garden!

'She would be very upset,' he thought, 'if she could see this … She would have a fit of coughing and pretend to be dying so that no one made fun of her. And, of course, I'd have to pretend to look after her, because otherwise – to make sure I was humiliated, too – she really would let herself die …'

Then he had another thought: 'I believed I'd been blessed with a unique flower, but all I had was a common-or-garden rose to add to my three knee-high volcanoes, one of which may actually be extinct. That doesn't make me a very grand prince …'

And he lay down on the grass and cried.

CHAPTER TWENTY-ONE

That was when the fox appeared.
'Hello,' said the fox.
'Hello,' replied the little prince politely,
but when he turned around, he didn't
see anyone.

'I'm over here,' said the voice, 'under the apple tree.'
'Who are you?' said the little prince. 'You're very
pretty …'
'I'm a fox,' said the fox.
'Come and play with me,' suggested the little
prince. 'I'm terribly unhappy …'

'I can't play with you,' said the fox. 'I haven't been tamed.'

'Oh, I'm sorry!' said the little prince.

But after thinking for a moment, he added, 'What does "tame" mean?'

'You're not from round here,' said the fox. 'What are you looking for?'

'I'm looking for people,' said the little prince. 'What does "tame" mean?'

'People,' said the fox, 'have guns and they hunt. It's a real nuisance! They also raise chickens. That's all they're interested in. Is it chickens you're looking for?'

'No,' said the little prince. 'I'm looking for friends. What does "tame" mean?'

'It's something most people have forgotten about,' said the fox. 'It means "creating a bond".'

'Creating a bond?'

'That's right,' said the fox. 'Right now, as far as I'm concerned, you're just a little boy like a hundred thousand other little boys. I don't need you and you don't need me, either. As far as you're concerned, I'm just a fox like a hundred thousand other foxes. But if you tame me, then we'll need each other. You'll be unique to me and I'll be unique to you …'

'I think I understand,' said the little prince. 'There's this flower … I think she's tamed me …'

'Quite possibly,' said the fox. 'All sorts of things happen on Earth …'

'Oh, no, she's not on Earth,' said the little prince.

The fox looked intrigued.

'On another planet?'

'Yes.'

'Are there hunters on this planet?'

'No.'

'Now that is interesting! And chickens?'

'No.'

'Nothing's perfect,' sighed the fox.

But this made him think again.

'I live a dull life. I hunt chickens. People hunt me. The chickens are all alike, and the people are all alike.

So I find it rather boring. But if you tame me, it'll be as if the sun has come out. Your footsteps will sound different from all the others. The others make me dive for cover. Yours will bring me out of my den, as if they were music. And look! You see those wheatfields over there? I don't eat bread, so wheat is of no use to me. Wheatfields mean nothing to me. Which is a pity! But you have golden hair, so, once you've tamed me, it'll be amazing! The golden wheat will remind me of you. And I'll love listening to the wind blowing through it …'

The fox fell silent and looked at the little prince for a while.

'Please … tame me!' he said.

'I'd like to,' replied the little prince, 'but I don't have much time. I have friends to find and lots of things to get to know.'

'You only know what you've tamed,' said the fox. 'People no longer have time to get to know anything. They buy everything ready-made from shops. But since there are no friend shops, people no longer have any friends. If you want a friend, tame me!'

'What do I have to do?' said the little prince.

'You have to be very patient,' replied the fox. 'First, you must sit quite a way away from me – about where you are now – on the grass. I'll look at you out of the corner of my eye and you'll say nothing. Talking causes misunderstandings. But, each day, you'll sit a little bit closer …'

The little prince came back the next day.

'It would have been better if you'd come back at the same time,' said the fox. 'If, for example, you come at four o'clock every afternoon, at three o'clock I'll start feeling excited. The later it gets, the more excited I'll be. By four o'clock, I'll be in a state of anxious anticipation. I'll be discovering the cost of happiness! But if you come whenever you feel like it, my heart won't know when to get ready ... It must be a ritual.'

'What's a ritual?' said the little prince.

'It's something most people have forgotten about,' said the fox. 'It's what makes one day different from another, one hour from another hour. Those hunters, for example, have a ritual. Every Thursday, they dance with the girls in the village. So Thursdays are wonderful! I can walk all the way to the vineyard. If the hunters went dancing whenever they felt like it, no day would be different, and I'd have no rest.'

So the little prince tamed the fox. And soon it was time for him to leave.

'Oh!' said the fox. 'I'm going to cry.'

'It's your fault,' said the little prince. 'I didn't mean you any harm, but you asked me to tame you.'

'That's right,' said the fox.

'But you're going to cry!' said the little prince.

'That's right,' said the fox.

'So you're no better off!'

'I am better off,' said the fox, 'because of the colour of the wheat.'

'Then he added, 'Go and look at the roses again. You'll realize that yours is unique. When you come back to say goodbye, I'll let you in on a secret.'

The little prince went to look at the roses again.

'You're not at all like my rose. You're nothing yet,' he told them, 'because no one has tamed you or been tamed by you. You're like my fox when I met him. He was just a fox like a hundred thousand other foxes. But I made friends with him, and now he's absolutely unique.'

And the roses felt uncomfortable.

'You're beautiful, but insignificant,' he went on. 'No one would die for you. Of course, anyone who didn't know would think my rose was just like you. But she alone is worth more than all of you because she's the one I've watered. Because she's the one I've covered with a dome. Because she's the one I've sheltered with a windbreak. Because she's the one I've killed caterpillars for (apart from the two or three I left to become butterflies). Because she's the one I've listened to when she has had something to complain, or boast, about – even sometimes when she has had nothing to say. Because she's my rose.'

And he went back to the fox.

'Goodbye,' he said.

'Goodbye,' said the fox. 'This is my secret. It's very simple. Only the heart sees clearly. The eyes don't see what's important.'

'The eyes don't see what's important,' repeated the little prince, so that he would remember.

'It's the time you've spent on your rose that makes your rose so precious.'

'It's the time I've spent on my rose …' said the little prince, so that he would remember.

'People have forgotten this simple truth,' said the fox, 'but you must remember it. Whatever you tame, you're responsible for. You're responsible for your rose …'

'I am responsible for my rose …' repeated the little prince, so that he would remember.

CHAPTER TWENTY-TWO

'Hello,' said the little prince.

'Hello,' said the signalman.

'What do you do?' said the little prince.

'I sort passengers into groups of a thousand,' said the signalman. 'I send the trains they're travelling on to the right or to the left.'

And, growling like thunder, a fast train flashed by, making the signal box shake.

'They're in a hurry,' said the little prince. 'Why?'

'They don't know – even the train driver doesn't know that,' said the signalman.

And a second train thundered by in the opposite direction.

'Why are they coming back so soon?' asked the little prince.

'They're not the same ones,' said the signalman. 'They're changing places.'

'Weren't they happy where they were?'

'People are never happy where they are,' said the signalman.

And a third train flashed by.

'Are they chasing the first group?' asked the little prince.

'They're not chasing anything,' said the signalman. 'They're asleep in there. Or falling asleep. Only the children press their noses to the windows.'

'Only children know what they're looking for,' said the little prince. 'They spend time on a rag doll, and it becomes precious to them. And if it's taken away from them, they cry ...'

'They're lucky,' said the signalman.

CHAPTER TWENTY-THREE

'Hello,' said the little prince.
'Hello,' said the salesman.
He was selling pills designed to quench the thirst.
'You take one of these per week and you no longer need to drink.'

'Why are you selling those?' said the little prince.

'They save a huge amount of time,' said the salesman. 'Experts have worked it out. You can save fifty-three minutes per week.'

'And what do you do with those fifty-three minutes?'

'Anything you like …'

'If I had fifty-three minutes to spare,' thought the little prince, 'I'd walk very slowly towards a drinking fountain …'

CHAPTER TWENTY-FOUR

It was now a week since my plane had come down in the desert, and I had listened to the story of the salesman as I drank the last drop of water I had left.

'Yes,' I said to the little prince, 'they're lovely, your stories, but I still haven't mended my plane, I've run out of water, and I, too, would be happy to be walking very slowly towards a drinking fountain!'

'My friend the fox ...' he began.

'Look, little fellow, this isn't about the fox!'

'Why?'

'Because we're going to die of thirst ...'

He didn't understand my argument and said, 'It's good to have had a friend, even if you're going to die. I'm very glad I had a fox for a friend ...'

He doesn't realize the danger we're in, I thought. He's never hungry or thirsty. A bit of sun is all he needs ...

But he looked at me, knowing what I was thinking.

'I'm thirsty, too ... Let's find a well ...'

I shrugged wearily. How ridiculous to think you will find a well in the middle of a vast desert. Nevertheless, we started walking.

We walked for hours in silence, until night fell and the stars began to shine. I thought I was imagining them, being almost delirious with thirst. The little prince's words were dancing in my head.

'So you're thirsty, too?' I asked him.

But he didn't answer my question.

He simply said, 'Water can be good for the heart as well …'

I didn't understand what that had to do with it, but I kept quiet. I knew very well there was no point in asking him to explain.

He was tired and sat down. I sat down next to him. And, after a while, he spoke again.

'The stars are beautiful because of an invisible flower …'

I said, 'That's right,' and looked in silence at the way the sand rippled in the moonlight.

'The desert is beautiful,' he added.

And it was true. I have always loved the desert. You sit on a sand dune and you see nothing. You hear nothing. And yet there is something radiant about the silence …

'What makes the desert more beautiful,' said the little prince, 'is that hidden somewhere in it is a well …'

To my surprise, I suddenly understood why the sand had this mysterious radiance. When I was a little boy, I lived in an old house, and it was said that treasure was buried beneath it. Of course, no one had ever been able to find it, or perhaps even looked for it, but it made the whole house magical. My house held a secret deep in its heart ...

'Yes,' I said to the little prince. 'Whether it's a house, the stars or the desert, what makes it beautiful is invisible!'

'I'm glad,' he said, 'that you agree with my fox.'

As the little prince fell asleep, I lifted him up and walked on, full of emotion. I felt I was carrying a fragile treasure. I even felt he was the most fragile thing on Earth. I looked at him in the moonlight – his forehead pale, his eyes closed, his curly hair trembling in the wind – and I thought, 'What I see is only a shell. What is most important is invisible ...'

His half-open lips seemed to be smiling, and I thought: 'What I find so touching about this sleeping prince is his loyalty to a flower, to a rose whose image shines within him like the flame in a lamp, even when he's asleep.' And that made him seem even more fragile. Lamps need protecting: a puff of wind can blow them out ...

And, walking on, I found the well at daybreak.

CHAPTER TWENTY-FIVE

'People throw themselves into trains,' said the little prince. But they've forgotten what they're looking for, so they rush around in circles …'

And he added, 'What's the point?'

The well we had come to wasn't like other Saharan wells. Saharan wells are simply holes in the sand. This one looked like a village well. But there was no village, and I thought I must be dreaming.

'That's strange,' I said. 'Everything's in place: the pulley, the rope, the bucket …'

He laughed as he touched the rope and spun the pulley. And the pulley squeaked like an old weather vane after a long lull.

'Listen,' said the little prince. 'We've woken the well and it's singing …'

I didn't want him to strain himself.

'Let me do it,' I said. 'It's too heavy for you.'

Slowly I hauled the bucket up to the mouth of the well. I secured it so that it hung straight. The pulley was still singing in my ears and the water still trembling. In it, I saw the sun tremble, too.

'I need this water,' said the little prince. 'Let me drink …'

And I understood what it was he had been looking for!

I lifted the bucket to his lips. He drank, without opening his eyes. It was like a silent celebration. The water had sprung from our walk beneath the stars, from the song of the pulley, from the effort of hauling it up. It was good for the heart, like a gift. When I was a little boy, it was the lights on the Christmas tree, the singing at midnight mass and the gently smiling faces around me that gave my Christmas presents their radiance.

'The people on your planet,' said the little prince, 'grow five thousand roses in a single garden ... but still they don't find what they're looking for ...'

'They don't,' I replied.

'... and yet what they're looking for can be found in a single rose or in a mouthful of water ...'

'That's right,' I said.

And the little prince added, 'You don't see with your eyes. You must look with your heart.'

I had drunk. I was breathing easily. The sand, at daybreak, is the colour of honey. That honey colour, too, made me happy. Why did I also have to be sad?

'You must keep your promise,' said the little prince gently as he sat down next to me again.

'What promise?'

'You know ... a muzzle for my little lamb ... I'm responsible for my flower!'

I put my hand in my pocket and took out my sketches. The little prince caught sight of them and laughed.

'Your baobabs look a bit like cabbages …'

'Oh!'

And I had been so proud of my baobabs!

'Your fox … its ears … they look a bit like horns … and they're too long!'

And he laughed again.

'That's not fair, little fellow. I'd only ever drawn boa constrictors with and without their insides showing.'

'Oh, it's all right!' he said. 'Children understand.'

So I sketched a muzzle. And my heart ached when I gave it to him.

'You're planning something but you're not telling me …'

But he didn't answer.

He said, 'You know, tomorrow it'll be a year since I landed on Earth …'

There was a silence.

Then he added, 'I came down just near here …'

And he blushed.

And once again, without knowing why, I felt a strange sadness. But a question occurred to me.

'So it was no accident that when I met you, a week ago, you were here in the desert, alone, a thousand miles from anywhere? You were going back to where you landed!'

The little price blushed again.

And I added, hesitantly, 'Was it because a year had passed? ...'

The little price blushed once more. He never answered questions, but blushing means 'Yes', doesn't it?

'Ah!' I said. 'Now I'm afraid ...'

But he said, 'You have work to do. You must go back to your machine now. I'll wait here for you. Come back tomorrow evening ...'

But his words did nothing to reassure me. I remembered the fox. You are likely to cry a little, once you have allowed yourself to be tamed ...

CHAPTER TWENTY-SIX

Next to the well were the remains of an ancient stone wall. On my way back the next evening, after finishing what I had to do, I saw my little prince sitting on top of it, with his legs dangling. And, even from a distance, I could hear him talking.

'Don't you remember?' he was saying. 'This isn't exactly the right place!'

Someone else must have replied to him, because he continued the conversation.

'No, no! It's the right day, but this is not the right place …'

I walked on towards the wall. I still couldn't see or hear anyone else. But the little prince responded again.

'… That's right. You'll see my footprints in the sand. Just wait for me by the first one. I'll be there tonight.'

I was twenty yards from the wall but I still couldn't see anyone.

After a moment's silence, the little prince went on, 'Is your venom good and strong? You're sure you won't make me suffer too much?'

My heart froze and I stopped in my tracks, but still I didn't understand.

'Now go away,' he said. 'I want to get down!'

I, too, looked down at the foot of the wall, and I jumped! There it was, its head raised towards the little prince – one of those yellow snakes that can kill you in thirty seconds. Thrusting my hand into my pocket to grab my revolver, I sprinted towards the wall, but, hearing me coming, the snake sank gently to the ground, like a fountain that has been turned off, and, quite slowly, slithered between the stones with a slightly metallic sound.

I reached the wall just in time to catch my little prince, whose face was as white as snow.

'What's going on? You're talking to snakes now?'

I had untied the golden scarf he always wore. I had splashed some water on his forehead and given him some to drink. I didn't dare ask him any more questions. He looked at me intently and put his arms around my neck. I felt his heart beating like a bird's before it dies, when it has been shot by a gun.

He said, 'I'm glad you've found what you needed to mend your machine. Now you'll be able to go home.'

'How did you know?'

I was just about to tell him that, much to my surprise, I'd managed to mend it!

He didn't answer my question, but added, 'I'm going home today, too.'

Then, in a sad voice, 'It's much farther … and much harder …'

I knew something extraordinary was happening. I held him tight like a little child, yet he seemed to be slipping straight down into a chasm, and there was nothing I could do to stop him …

His face was serious and he was staring distractedly into the distance.

'I've got your lamb. And I've got its box. And I've got its muzzle …'

And he smiled sadly.

I stood still for a long time. I could tell he was gradually recovering.

'You're frightened, little prince …'

He had certainly had a fright! But he laughed gently.

'I'll be much more frightened tonight …'

Once again my blood froze at the thought of something irreparable. And I realized I couldn't bear the prospect of never hearing that laugh again. A laugh that was like a fountain in the desert.

'Little prince, let me hear your laugh again …'

But he said, 'Tonight it'll be exactly a year. My star will be directly over the place where I came down last year …'

'Little prince, tell me I only dreamed the story about the snake and your meeting him under the star …'

But he didn't reply.

He just said, 'What's important can't be seen.'

'That's right …'

'It's the same with my flower. If you love a flower that's up there in the stars, you enjoy looking at the night sky. Every star has a flower.'

'That's right …'

'It's the same with the water. The water you gave me to drink was like music because of the pulley and the rope … Remember how good it was?'

'That's right …'

'At night, you'll look at the stars. My planet is too small for you to see. It's better that way. For you, it will be somewhere among the stars. So you'll love looking at all the stars … They'll all be your friends. And I shall give you a present …'

He laughed again.

'Oh, little prince, little prince, I love hearing your laugh!'

'Yes, it'll be my present to you … and it'll be like the water …'

'What do you mean?'

'The stars aren't the same for everyone. For some, they're guides to help them travel. For others, they're nothing but specks of light. For those who study them, they're a puzzle. For my businessman, they were lumps of gold. But for all of them, the stars are silent. Your stars will be like no one else's …'

'What do you mean?'

'When you look up at the sky at night, because you know that I'll be somewhere among them and that I'll be laughing, for you it'll be as if all the stars are laughing. You, and only you, will be able to hear the stars laugh!'

And he laughed again.

'And when you've got over your sadness (people always get over sadness), you'll be glad you met me. You'll always be my friend. You'll feel like laughing with me. And sometimes you'll simply open the window, just for fun … And your friends will wonder why on earth you're laughing at the sky. So you'll tell them, "Yes, the stars always make me laugh!" And they'll think you're mad. I'll have played a really good trick on you …'

And he laughed again.

'It'll be as if, instead of laughing stars, I'd given you millions of laughing jingle bells …'

And he laughed again. Then he was serious once more.

'Tonight … you know … you mustn't come.'

'I won't leave you.'

'It'll look as if I'm sick … almost as if I'm dying. That's what happens. I don't want you to see that. There's no point …'

'I won't leave you.'

But something was worrying him.

'I say that … partly because of the snake. I don't want him to bite you … Snakes are nasty.

They can bite for no reason …'

'I won't leave you.'

But something had reassured him.

'That's true – they don't have any venom left for the second bite, do they?'

That night, I didn't see him leave. He had slipped away silently. When I caught up with him, he was walking briskly and determinedly.

All he said was, 'Oh, it's you …'

And he took my hand. But he was still worrying.

'You shouldn't have come. You'll get upset. It'll look as though I'm dead, but I won't be …'

I said nothing.

'You see, it's too far. I can't take my body with me. It's too heavy.'

I said nothing.

'It'll just be like an old shell that has been cast off. There's nothing sad about old shells …'

I said nothing.

He was losing heart, but he tried again.

'It'll be gentle, you'll see. I'll be looking at the stars, too. And every star will be a well with a rusty pulley. Every star will be a fountain I can drink from …'

I said nothing.

'It'll be such fun! You'll have five hundred million jingle bells, and I'll have five hundred million wells …'

And he fell silent, too, because he was crying.

'It's here. Let me go on alone.'

And he sat down because he was frightened.

Again he spoke.

'You know ... my flower ... I'm responsible for her! And she's so fragile! And she's so naive. She has four puny thorns to protect her against the world ...'

I also sat down, because my legs would no longer support me.

He said, 'That's it … That's all there is to say …'
He hesitated a moment longer, then stood up.
He stepped forwards. I was unable to move.

All I saw was a yellow flash near his ankle. He didn't move for a moment. He didn't cry out. Then he fell gently, like a felled tree. There was not even a sound as he dropped to the sand.

CHAPTER TWENTY-SEVEN

And now, of course, it is six years later … I have never told anyone this story before. When I got back, the other men were happy to see me alive. I was sad, but I told them it was because I was tired …

Now I have more or less got over it. I mean … not completely. But I know he made it back to his planet because, the next morning, his body was no longer there. It wasn't so heavy after all … And at night, I love listening to the stars. They are like five hundred million jingle bells …

But I must tell you something extraordinary. You remember the muzzle I drew for the little prince? Well, I forgot to add a leather strap! He would never have been able to put it on the lamb. So I keep wondering, 'What has happened up there? Maybe the lamb has eaten the flower after all …'

Sometimes I think, 'Definitely not! The little prince puts the glass dome over his flower every night, and he keeps a close eye on his lamb …' That makes me happy. And the stars all laugh sweetly.

But sometimes I think, 'We all get distracted now and then, and that's all it needs! One evening he forgot the dome, or else the lamb got out of its box …' And then the jingle bells all turn to tears!

It is one of the great mysteries. Those of you who love the little prince as I do will know that the whole universe is different according to whether, in some unknown part of it, a lamb we have never seen has, or has not, eaten a rose …

Look at the sky and ask yourself, 'Has the lamb eaten the flower – yes or no?' And you will see how everything changes …

And no grown-up will ever understand how important that is!

For me, this is the most beautiful and most desolate landscape in the world. It is the same landscape as the one on the previous page, but I have drawn it again to make sure you have taken it in. It is the place where the little prince appeared on Earth, and then disappeared.

Look closely at it to make sure you recognize it if ever you should go to Africa and find yourself in the desert. And if you happen to come across it, please, don't hurry. Stop for a moment directly beneath the star! And if a little boy comes towards you, and if he is laughing and has hair the colour of gold and doesn't answer your questions, you will know exactly who he is. If so, think of me and comfort me! Write to me at once and tell me he is back ...

THE END